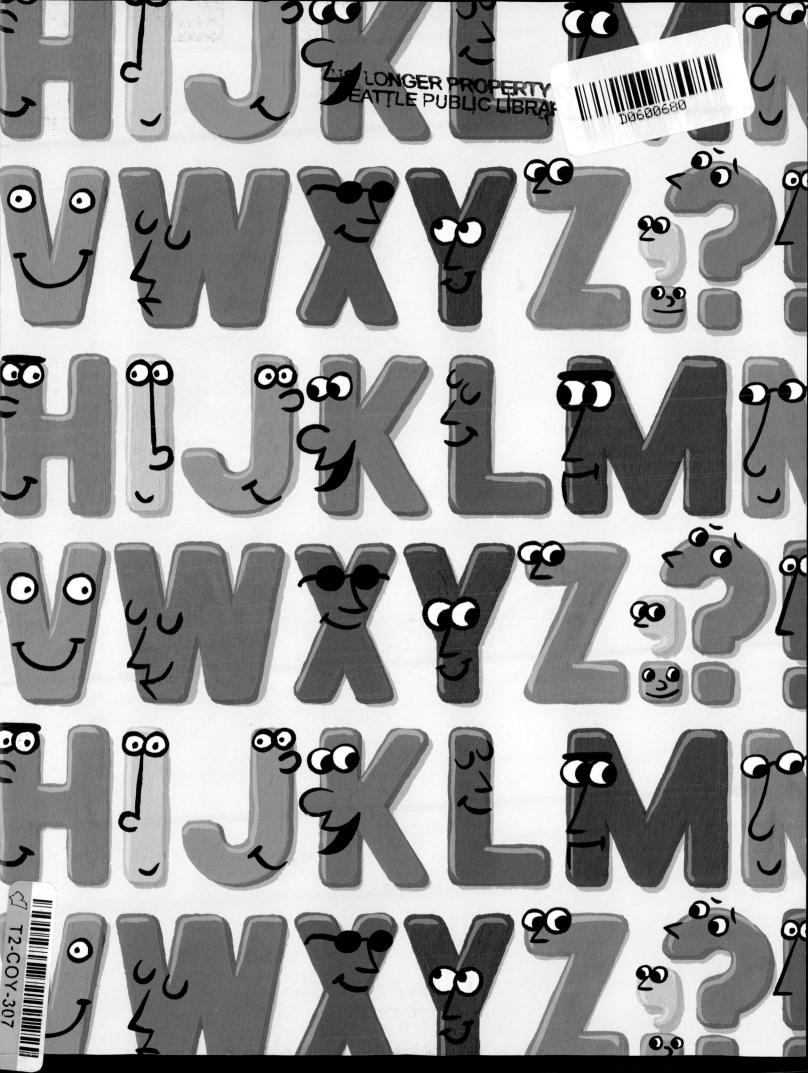

Y I E A RD?

CARON LEVIS
PICTURES BY ANDY RASH

FARRAR STRAUS GIROUX ▪ NEW YORK

Once upon a refrigerator, the letters of the alphabet gathered together to tell a story.

WHOM

should our story be about?

wondered W.

How about a **CAT?**

suggested C.

What about a

KITTEN?

exclaimed K.

MILK

"A CAPTAIN!"

"A KING!"

"A CASHEW!"

"A KID!"

Soon the refrigerator was
CROWDED with CHARACTERS.

"May I have a word with you?" K said to C.
"I wish you'd quit stealing my sound."

C was confused. "*Your* sound?"

"Everybody knows the K sound is *my* sound. Every time you start one of *my* K words, you just CONFUSE everybody!" said K.

"Why can't we share?" asked C.
"Because you keep taking all the good words!" said K. "Like CASTLE and CLOUDS!"

"But you get KITE!"
pointed out C.

"You get CRASH!" said K.
"And CRACK!"

"Well—but you get . . . um . . . KIWIS! And KISSES!"

"So what? You get CARROTS and CUDDLES!"

"Oh, that's true. I do like CARROTS and CUDDLES," said C.

"See?" said K. "You get CAKE and CARTWHEELS and CARNIVALS, and the worst part is, you get to start all of the . . .

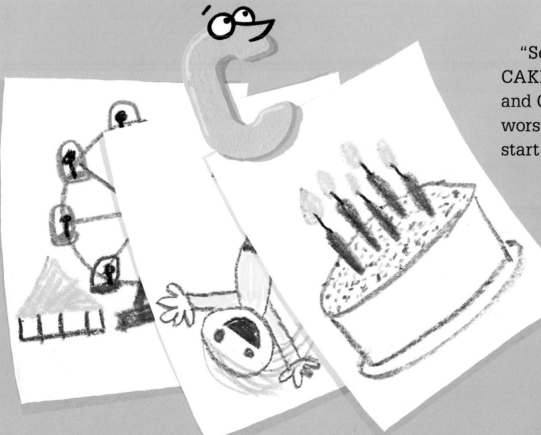

. . . CARS!"

"I do?" said C. "COOL!"

"Argh, you get COOL, too!" groaned K.

"Stop COMPLAINING," grumbled C.

"But it isn't fair!"

"Well, it's not my fault!"

"I don't want to stand next to you anymore!"

"I don't want to stand next to you either!"

C and K stormed off to separate sides
of the refrigerator.
They both felt very

The other letters were worried.
If C and K wouldn't stand together, there
wouldn't be any more DUCKS to QUACK.

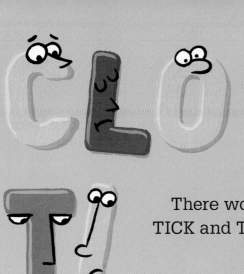

There wouldn't be any CLOCKS to TICK and TOCK.

There wouldn't be any SOCKS!

There wouldn't be any
SMOCKS or BLOCKS!
No STICKS or LICKS!

No ROCKETS or POCKETS or PICKLES!

The world would be
quite out of LUCK.

No one knew how to get C and K BACK together.

"You know, I would give you more words to start if I COULD," called C, "but I CAN'T."

"I don't want to talk about it," sighed K. "In fact, I don't want to talk at all."

K fell silent.

Which gave N an idea.

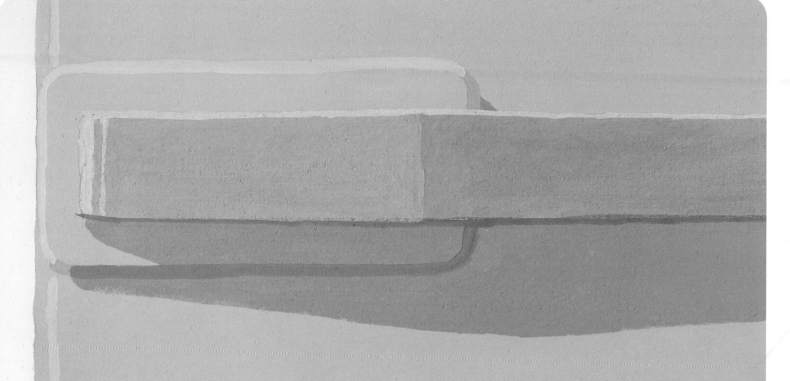

"May I have a word with you?" N asked K.

K didn't answer.

"You don't have to make a sound," said N. "Just let me stand here next to you."

They shuffled together. Soon, they started a story . . .

. . . about a

KNIGHT

who kept
getting

KNOTS

in his

KNITTING.

All the letters gathered
around to help—all
except C, who was still
in the CORNER, looking
CRUSHED.

 felt terrible.

 comes next?

wondered W.
The letters thought and thought . . .

said K.

C, may I have a word with you?

C wasn't sure.

I'm sorry I was so

before. I have an idea, but I need you.

C was

The two letters shuffled toward each other. CLOSER and CLOSER.

Soon the **KNIGHT** had **KNOTS** in the **KNITTING** of his . . .

The letters laughed and laughed.

HA! That was

said H.

They decided to try another story.

should it be about this time?

wondered W.

said the other letters, worried.

But now C and K

how to

So, once upon a refrigerator, there was a . . .

KITTEN in a CAPE,

For Emily, who showed me
that Sharing starts with Sisters.

And N is for Nina and Novick,
with special thanks to Nathaniel
for gifting the keys to this car.
—C.L.

For Nate and Alex.
—A.R.

Farrar Straus Giroux Books for Young Readers
An imprint of Macmillan Publishing Group, LLC
175 Fifth Avenue, New York 10010

Text copyright © 2017 by Caron Levis
Illustrations copyright © 2017 by Andy Rash
All rights reserved

Color separations by Embassy Graphics
Printed in China by RR Donnelley Asia Printing Solutions Ltd.,
Dongguan City, Guangdong Province
Designed by Andrew Arnold
First edition, 2017
1 2 3 4 5 6 7 8 9 10

mackids.com

Library of Congress Cataloging-in-Publication Data

Names: Levis, Caron, author. | Rash, Andy, illustrator.
Title: May I have a word? / Caron Levis ; pictures by Andy Rash.
Description: First edition. | New York : Farrar Straus Giroux, 2017. |
   Summary: The letters C and K have an argument when K accuses C of stealing
   all the good words that start with the "k" sound.
Identifiers: LCCN 2016035961 | ISBN 9780374348809 (hardcover)
Subjects: | CYAC: Alphabet—Fiction. | Vocabulary—Fiction.
Classification: LCC PZ7.C579695 May 2017 | DDC [E]—dc23
LC record available at https://lccn.loc.gov/2016035961

Our books may be purchased in bulk for promotional, educational, or business use.
Please contact your local bookseller or the Macmillan Corporate and Premium Sales Department
at (800) 221-7945 ext. 5442 or by e-mail at MacmillanSpecialMarkets@macmillan.com.

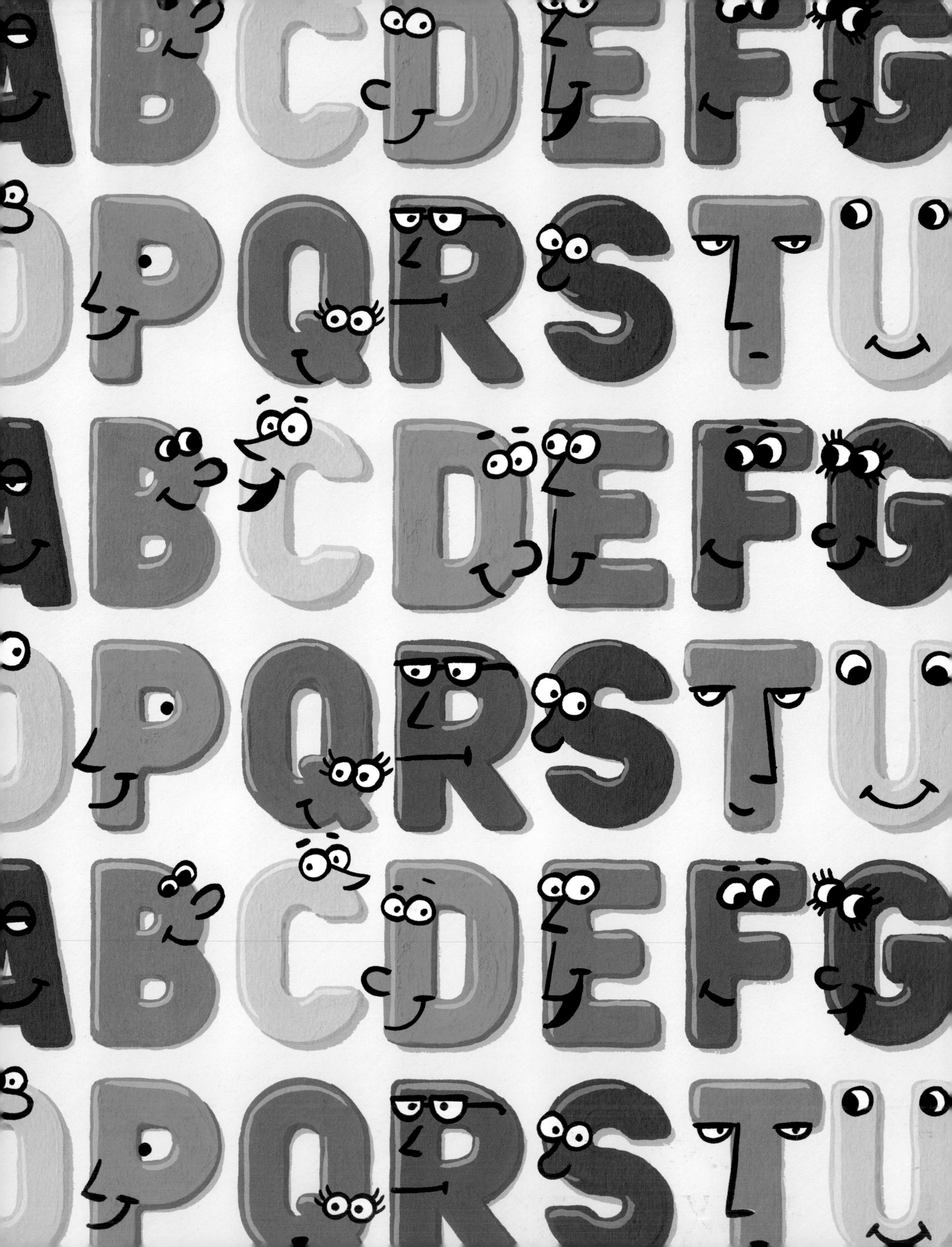
BCDEFG
PQRSTU
BCDEFG
PQRSTU
BCDEFG
PQRSTU